Ducks Don't Wear Socks

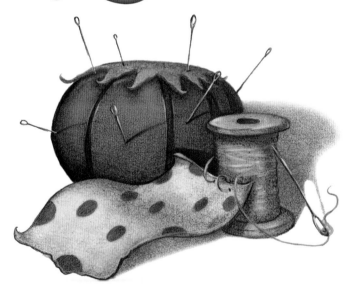

BY John Nedwidek

ILLUSTRATED BY Lee White

Viking

VIKING
Published by Penguin Group
Penguin Young Readers Group, 345 Hudson Street, New York, New York 10014, U.S.A.
Penguin Group (Canada), 90 Eglinton Avenue East, Suite 700, Toronto,
Ontario, Canada M4P 2Y3 (a division of Pearson Penguin Canada Inc.)
Penguin Books Ltd, 80 Strand, London WC2R 0RL, England
Penguin Ireland, 25 St Stephen's Green, Dublin 2,
Ireland (a division of Penguin Books Ltd)
Penguin Group (Australia), 250 Camberwell Road, Camberwell,
Victoria 3124, Australia (a division of Pearson Australia Group Pty Ltd)
Penguin Books India Pvt Ltd, 11 Community Centre,
Panchsheel Park, New Delhi – 110 017, India
Penguin Group (NZ), 67 Apollo Drive, Rosedale, North Shore 0632,
New Zealand (a division of Pearson New Zealand Ltd.)
Penguin Books (South Africa) (Pty) Ltd, 24 Sturdee Avenue,
Rosebank, Johannesburg 2196, South Africa

Penguin Books Ltd, Registered Offices: 80 Strand, London WC2R 0RL, England

First published in 2008 by Viking, a division of Penguin Young Readers Group

LIBRARY OF CONGRESS CATALOGING-IN-PUBLICATION DATA
Nedwidek, John.
Ducks don't wear socks / by John Nedwidek ; illustrated by Lee White.
p. cm.
Summary: Emily, a serious girl, meets a duck who helps her see the more humorous side of life.
ISBN 978-0-670-06136-5 (hardcover)
Special Markets ISBN 978-0-670-01193-3 Not for Resale
[1. Ducks—Fiction. 2. Humorous stories.] I. White, Lee, date– ill. II. Title. III. Title: Ducks do not wear socks.
PZ7.N327Du 2008
[E]—dc22
2007023122

Manufactured in China
Set in ITC Cheltenham
Book design by Sam Kim

This Imagination Library edition is published by Penguin Group (USA), a Pearson
company, exclusively for Dolly Parton's Imagination Library, a not-for-profit
program designed to inspire a love of reading and learning, sponsored in part by The
Dollywood Foundation. Penguin's trade editions of this work are available wherever
books are sold.

Emily was a serious girl.

One day, while she was in a serious mood,
taking a serious walk, she met Duck.

Duck was definitely not serious.

"Duck," asked Emily. "What are you wearing?"

"Socks!" yelled Duck.

"Ducks don't wear socks," replied Emily, quite seriously.

"Cold feet!" yelled Duck, and off he went.

The next day, they met again. Emily was still serious. Duck was still not.

"No socks!" laughed Duck.

"But," Emily pointed out, quite earnestly, "you're wearing a tie . . . and ducks don't wear ties."

"Big meeting!" yelled Duck. And off he ran, tie flapping in the wind.

The day after, Emily was still a serious girl, but she almost smiled when she saw Duck again.

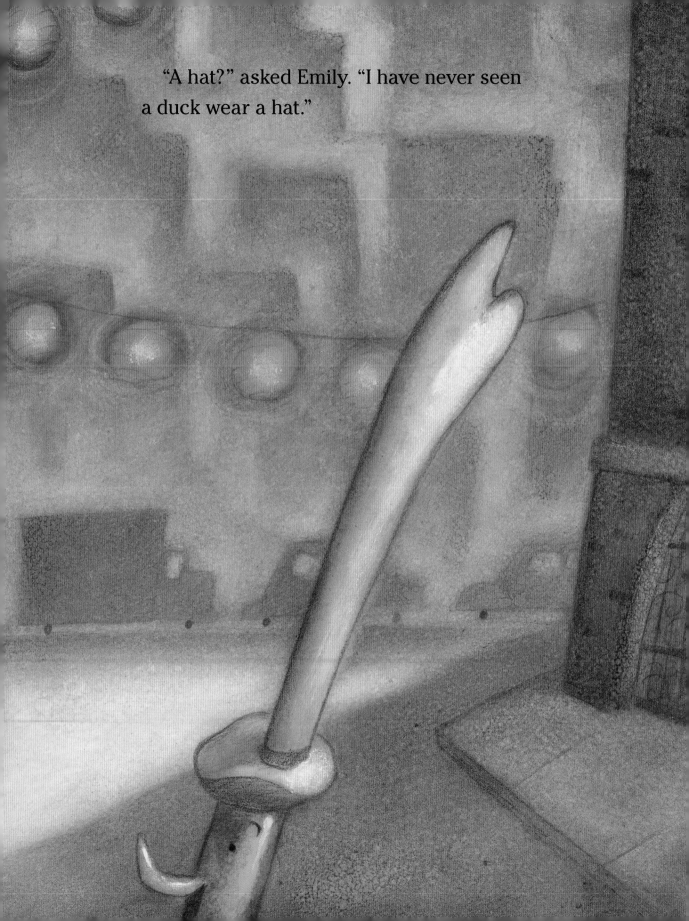

"A hat?" asked Emily. "I have never seen a duck wear a hat."

"Late for the roundup!" yelled Duck. And off he galloped, into the sunset.

Emily almost laughed, but she bit her lip and managed to stay serious.

Until the next day . . .

"Duck!" Emily began to ask. "Are those . . . ?"

"Boots!" yelled Duck. "Fields to plow! Crops to plant!"

Emily's lips slowly curled into a smile, and she kept smiling until the next day when . . .

"Duck!" exclaimed Emily, at the sight of Duck wearing . . .

"Underwear!" yelled Duck.

"I have never, ever seen a duck wearing underwear!" Emily gasped.

"Pants on the line!" yelled Duck. And off he
sailed, not the least bit embarrassed.
Emily smiled. And she began to giggle.

Before she went to sleep that night, Emily
laughed—just a little bit—to herself.

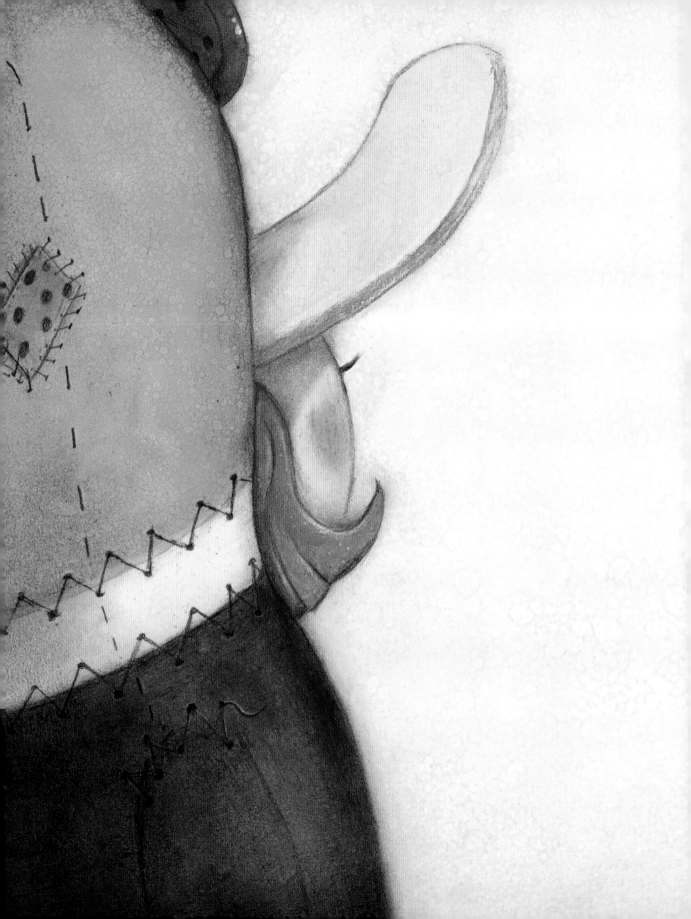

The next day, Emily just happened to meet Duck.
Again.
But this time . . .
"Emily!" called Duck. "What are you wearing?"

"I'm a **duck!**" laughed Emily.

"A duck!" yelled Duck.

Emily laughed so hard that she cried.

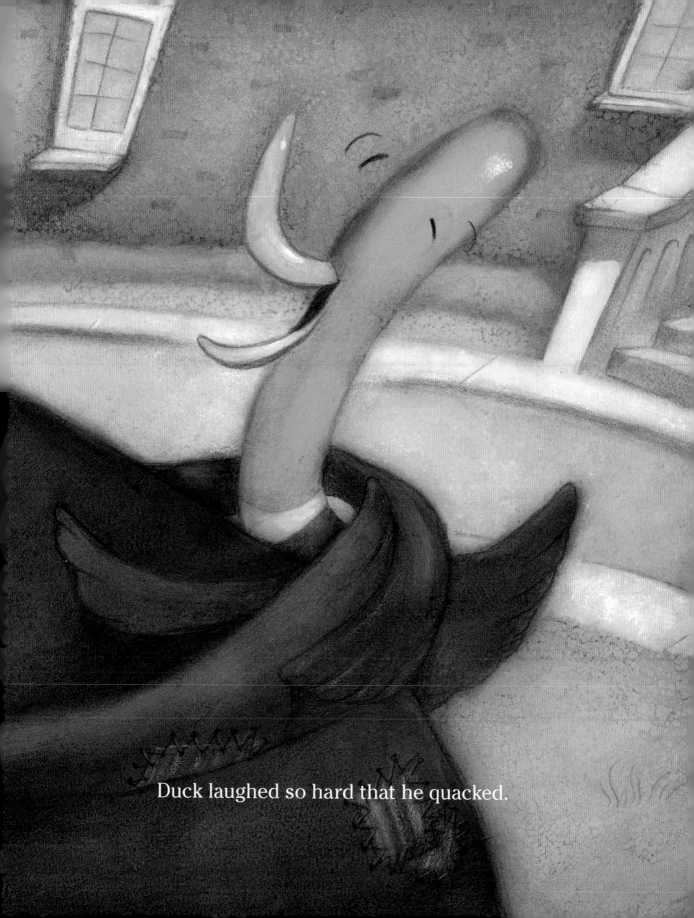

Duck laughed so hard that he quacked.

And off they went.